At the Park

written by
Karen Hoenecke
illustrated by
Bruce Biddle

KAEDEN ❤ BOOKS™

I slide down the slide.

I dig in the sand.

I swing on the swing.

I hold Daddy's hand.

We get the picnic basket.

We eat in the park.

We hurry home quickly
before it gets dark.